The PS Brothers

Maribeth Boelts

Harcourt

Houghton Mifflin Harcourt

Boston   New York   2010

Harcourt is an imprint of Houghton Mifflin Harcourt Publishing Company.

www.hmhbooks.com

The text of this book is set in Meridien.
Book Design by Regina Roff

Library of Congress Cataloging-in-Publication Data
Boelts, Maribeth, 1964–
The PS Brothers / Maribeth Boelts.
p. cm.
Summary: Sixth-graders Russell and Shawn, poor and picked on, work together scooping dog droppings to earn money for a rottweiler puppy to protect them from bullies, but when they learn the puppies' owner is running an illegal dogfighting ring, they are torn about how to respond.
ISBN 978-0-547-34249-8 (hardcover : alk. paper) [1. Dogs—Fiction. 2. Moneymaking projects—Fiction. 3. Bullies—Fiction. 4. Dogfighting—Fiction. 5. Conduct of life—Fiction. 6. Uncles—Fiction.] I. Title.
PZ7.B6338Pac 2010
[Fic]—dc22
2009049975

Manufactured in the United States of America
DOC 10 9 8 7 6 5 4 3 2 1
4500251688

For my extraordinary partners,
editor Samantha McFerrin and agent
Scott Treimel. And for Will, my inspiration.

"I do not wish to treat friendships daintily, but with the
roughest courage."—Ralph Waldo Emerson

Chapter One

...

It started with a pooper-scooper.

"Check it out, Russell. I got it for a buck at a junk sale," Shawn said, scratching a mosquito bite on his bony shin. His fingernails were orange from the cheez-whirlz he's always eating. He squeezed the handle of the pooper-scooper, and the scoop opened and closed. He looked at me and said, "Cool, huh?"

I finished the last slurp of my blue raspberry slush and glanced at Shawn's find. Blue raspberry slushes were a habit I funded by collecting returnable pop cans on the way to school. I stuffed them into my backpack. Then after school I cashed them in at the DX gas station. The good thing was that I was able to buy the blue raspberry slushes. The bad thing was that my backpack, along with my homework, was always sticky from the cans. Sticky homework is a big deal when you're in sixth grade and your teacher is constantly washing her hands and spraying your desk with disinfectant, like you had the plague or something.

"I don't know if you've noticed," I said to Shawn. "Neither of us have a dog."

"Not right now, anyway, but we will pretty soon, and if a dog eats, he poops. Then you'll be glad I had money today to get this scooper. I almost paid the new kid to give me half of his pizza burger at lunch today, but it's a good thing I didn't."

I shrugged. It was hard to see Shawn so excited about us getting a dog to share, because it wasn't going to happen. I hadn't given up on it altogether, but I knew some dreams are better kept in a box, where a kid can visit them once in a while, and so they can't peck at him like a bunch of crazed baby ducks.

All summer long, it had been a quest. I practically lived at the Wade County Public Library, reading books about dogs. I ate up books about Seeing Eye dogs, dogs who rescued boys off mountains, dogs who ate the apple pie at the family reunion, and dogs who played quarterback in the big game.

I yawned through books about sappy dogs that would lick the tears off some girl's face, and goofball dogs that ran through the house covered in soapsuds. I had read about them all—heroic dogs, hilarious dogs, and jock dogs who could find their way home through a blizzard.

When I finished with the fiction books, I holed up in the corner of the library where the homeless guys sit and fall asleep behind their newspapers. There, I read nonfiction and tried to squeeze into my brain all that stuff about teaching a dog not to pee in your house, jump up on your grandma, or tear apart your shoes.

But the reason I started giving up on the quest was because in all that reading, I hadn't found a word about the kind of dog Shawn and I wanted. We wanted a mean one—not mean to us, but to anyone who tried to mess with us, take stuff from us, or say bad things about our families. A dog that would sniff out danger like it was sniffing out a bone, and fight to his death to protect us. It wouldn't go hiding from trouble, either. The dog we wanted would jump right in the middle and take care of it—with its teeth.

Shawn hung out at the library, too, but he didn't do any reading. He was too much in love with Deb, one of the ladies who worked there.

"Did you see her toenails, Russell?" he asked. "She has some kind of fancy painted toenails with little star stickers on them, and she wears those flip-floppy shoes and talks all nice and everything.

I've been thinking about it, and I think she might like me, too."

"How do you know that?"

"Well . . . there's the way she answers my questions in that whispery voice," Shawn said dreamily. "I ask her about what kinds of stuff kids ate a hundred years ago, and she goes on and on about their lunch pails, and how they carried baked potatoes in their pockets on the way to school, and how they only got one piece of candy at Christmas, and what butchering a hog was like. Sometimes she gets books out for me and shows me the pictures so I can see what she's talking about."

Shawn had a thing about food. He talked about it, dreamed about it, and tied every adventure and everyone he met to it. Everything went back to food.

"It's her job to answer your questions," I said. "And she whispers because she's in a library."

But I knew Shawn was right in some weird way, too. Deb wasn't in love with him, but she liked both of us. When I was at the library the entire day, my stomach growling right through lunch, it was Deb who noticed. She'd walk by all casual and hand me off a granola bar or some graham crackers, even though there's not supposed to be any eating in the library. She didn't make a big deal about it, or smile in that almost-crying way like she was doing something special for a poor kid, or ask me questions about why I wasn't going home for lunch. I'd thank her with a quick smile. I didn't want the homeless guys to feel bad, so once they were asleep, I'd raise my book to cover my mouth and snack away.

When we weren't at the library that summer, we spent a long time in the camper parked in my Uncle Cory's backyard. The camper was supposed to be a "pop-up," but it was so old it didn't pop up without a ton of work. Two people had to use all their arm muscles to crank the rusty handle near the bottom of the trailer part of the camper. This made the dented, flat roof go up. Then, they had to stand on opposite sides of the camper, pulling and jiggling the canvas sides until they slid out on their rusty tracks. There were beds in each of these sides, with lumpy foam pads that smelled like the boys' locker room at school on a hot day. Inside the camper, I sat on an orange plaid bench seat that opened for storage and ate at a rickety green table. There was also a cupboard, and a dusty sink with no water hooked up. If you unzipped the openings in the canvas walls, you had fabric screens. One of the screens had a hole that I repaired with a Band-Aid to keep the mosquitoes out. Unless it was roasting hot outside, I kept the windows zipped.

I moved into the camper after my dad got arrested for robbing the Flying Eagle Mini Mart. The paper said he told the lady behind the counter that he had a gun. I knew the truth. He didn't own a gun, but he was real good at faking it, with a fist in his sweatshirt pocket and a hard expression on his face, like a guy might look if he did have a gun. The lady believed him. She gave my dad a wad of bills with one hand and pushed the police alarm under the counter with the other. When the police arrested him, he told them to take me to his little brother Cory's house so I'd be looked after. Looked after for a long while, since this robbery was his second offense.

I barely knew Uncle Cory when I was dropped off. The last time I had seen him was six years before, at my mom's funeral. I was five years old. What I remember about him from the funeral is that he didn't say anything about how my mom died—how her old van blew a tire on the interstate, then rolled, then crashed into a pole, all on her way home from work. He also didn't talk to me about angels or heaven or my mom watching over me, like all the other grownups did.

What he did do was stand next to me at the funeral home. He got me a paper cup filled with orange drink. He tied my shoes and showed me a cool spider web in the corner. And all he said was that my mom sure loved me and that it would be okay . . . and that made me feel better than angels or anything else.

But right after the funeral, he and my dad had a nasty argument, and they stopped talking. Pretty soon my memory of Uncle Cory at the funeral home got squashed by all the crazy stories my dad told me about him. Uncle Cory, according to my dad, had a fighting streak, a dog-hating streak, and a bunch of other streaks. Because of those stories, and him being almost a stranger, I chose to sleep in his camper rather than his house.

"It gets real hot in the summer," Uncle Cory had warned me when I first asked him about the camper. "And you'll freeze in the winter. Wind is bad, too, and yeah, it leaks when it rains. If you sleep in the house, the couch pulls out into a bed at least."

Before I picked the camper, I needed to ask a question. I tried to be the tough guy and keep my voice from sounding like the answer mattered much, even though it really did.

"Does the door lock?"

Uncle Cory laughed like he was sort of embarrassed. "Sure it locks—unless you do this." Then he gave that locked door a tug, and it opened right up. My stomach dropped. From that day on, I propped an old chair under the handle when I went to bed—and hoped that if there were a killer out there, he wouldn't have any muscles, or any arms for that matter.

The camper, even with its problems, made for a good place to hang out with Shawn and talk about our dream dog.

"He'll need way long fangs," Shawn said, picking my dirty socks up off the camper floor with the pooper-scooper.

"Fangs are good," I agreed. "Big is good, too— like ninety pounds."

"Yeah. Three times what I weigh," Shawn said.

"Something like that," I said, knowing that Shawn had done the math wrong, unless he hadn't grown since he was in preschool. Math and Shawn don't go together, and neither does reading and Shawn. Or school and Shawn for that matter. No use rubbing it in.

"He's gotta have a spiked collar," I offered. "A black one with his name in silver letters."

"Oh yeah." Shawn stretched out on the camper bed, pushed up on the camper canvas with his bare feet, and let it flop back down with a heavy *thwack*. "What'll we name him?"

"We'll know his name when we see him, but it better be something vicious."

We talked until suppertime, but we weren't the kind of kids who had a real suppertime. I remembered seeing movies where mothers called their kids in to eat or get ready for bed. Across some corner baseball field, kids would run on home, all excited and out of breath, ready to sit down and eat mashed potatoes and maybe meatloaf, and drink a giant glass of milk. Then they'd tell their father all about their day. Shawn's and my suppertime didn't look like anything in the movies.

"Want a sandwich?" I asked.

"Make me two." Shawn sat up, his curly brown hair flattening against the droopy canvas roof.

I lifted the top of the bench seat in the camper. There was half a loaf of white bread and a jar of Spanish peanut butter. It looked like peanut butter, but the label said MANTEQUILLA DE CACAHUETE. It was in the sale cart at the dollar store, and after cashing in my pop cans at the DX, I had enough money to buy a jar for eighty-five cents. It was a good thing that not everything at the dollar store was a dollar. Uncle Cory always left me something in the fridge before he went to work—a burrito, a piece of pizza, grilled cheese—so I could have eaten inside, but it was better to be on my own. I didn't feel like depending on anybody for anything, since it hadn't worked out for me before.

"Whatcha got to drink?" Shawn asked.

"Just the drinking fountain."

Shawn shrugged. There was a short hose hooked up to the side of Uncle Cory's house. That was the drinking fountain, as long as Uncle Cory's water was still turned on. When the city turned it off because he couldn't pay the bill, then we got a drink at the neighbor's hose. You had to be fast to do that 'cause people can hear when their water is going. Slurp and run.

After supper Shawn grabbed his pooper-scooper and we went out looking for a stray ninety-pound dog with a spiked collar and long fangs. Maybe some kid had let one go, or it ran away, or maybe the owner moved and forgot to take his ninety-pound dog along. You never knew.

I climbed onto Shawn's bike and Shawn climbed on behind, grabbing the back of my shirt. I stood up to ride. Some kid said it was against the law to ride double, but no cop had stopped us yet. In my neighborhood, they had other stuff to worry about.

We wove our way down the bumpy street and through the puddles in the alley. We saw stray cats every once in a while, but most of the dogs were either in their houses, on chains, or in kennels in the backyards. We stopped and petted the dogs that were outside, if they seemed friendly. We didn't know their real names, so Shawn and I named them ourselves . . .

Old Lardo, the fat dog.

Blinkie, the one-eyed dog.

Coyote, the howler.

Diggety, whose yard looked like a minefield.

No stray dogs.

We rode around awhile more—through the school playground, behind the junkyard. It was then that Shawn spotted something.

"Russell! Look over there!" he yelled, and gave the back of my shorts a yank so hard to the right I crashed the bike into a street sign, sending Shawn flying. The handlebar twisted and gave me a hard poke in the gut.

"What're you doing? Man, if you wanted me to stop, tell me. Don't just go pulling—"

Shawn interrupted. "Russ—take a look at that sign!"

In a bald patch on a front yard there was a homemade sign with the words PUREBRED ROTT-WEILER PUPPIES—$200.

I wheeled the bike over and chucked it to the ground, leaving its front tire spinning. Two cars were pulled up in the yard—both hoods open, tools beside them. Maybe this guy needed money to fix his cars and would give us a good deal. Maybe there was a sale today, kind of like the Spanish peanut butter. We had to find out.

Shawn pushed me to go ahead of him, and we walked up onto a raggedy porch. Any wrong step, and we'd fall right through. I knocked on the screen door, not too hard and not too soft. We hadn't imagined a puppy, only a dog. But a dream has to start somewhere, and maybe this was it.

Chapter Two

...

The guy looked like he could be Jesus' evil twin.

I'd seen pictures of Jesus at church. The church
bus stopped outside Uncle Cory's house, and the
driver promised doughnuts and orange juice to any
kid who would hop on and come to church on
Sundays. For a doughnut, I'd do mostly anything.
And I'd definitely go to Sunday school, even though
I was the oldest kid there and just about the only
boy, depending on the week. I sat on a little plastic
chair meant for a baby and kept my head down. If

you looked a Sunday school teacher in the eyes, or even in her direction, she'd call on you.

"This is Jesus," the lady who taught the class would say in this smiley, slow voice, and she'd point to the cover of a Jesus coloring book. The coloring-book Jesus had long brown hair, kind of wavy like a girl's, and a sort of nice, sleepy smile. His hands were stretched out in front of him, like if someone gave him a watermelon, he'd be ready for it. He had on a white robe with nothing spilled on it, and sandals, too.

Then she'd ask the same questions. It didn't take me long to figure out that there were only three answers to most of the questions Sunday school teachers asked.

"Boys and girls, who made the world?" (God)

"And who was God's Son?" (Jesus)

"How does that make you feel?" (Happy)

If you said the three answers, you got a piece of gum. One Sunday a month, puppets would ask the questions, and that was even more embarrassing.

In the puppet show, there was a boy puppet with green overalls and freckles that were too big, and there was an annoying, know-it-all girl puppet. The boy puppet was always getting into trouble. The girl puppet had all the answers. Both puppets were operated by grownups who didn't even try to hide inside the refrigerator-box puppet theater. And no matter what the story was—whether the boy puppet stole a cookie from the cookie jar or didn't want to go to church because he got a new toy rocket he wanted to play with—the answers circled back to "God," "Jesus," and "Happy."

What those Sunday school teachers didn't know was that I talked to God a lot, and the guy who owned the camper before Uncle Cory had left a Bible in one of the drawers. I had written my name in it and had read some parts of it. Even with all that, I still hated Sunday school. But because of the gum, doughnuts, and juice, and maybe because I thought that God would be more likely to help me out when I asked him, I said the three words. I sat on the baby chair. I clapped for the puppet show.

This guy at the screen door was sort of like that coloring-book Jesus, but with sideburns. His long hair was stringy, and his mouth didn't have a nice, sleepy smile—his mouth had a cigarette. He had on a gray muscle shirt, and one arm looked like he'd dipped it in a bucket of tattoo.

"Yeah?" he said. I could hear a dog barking in the background—the kind of barking a dog does when he's thinking about ripping somebody's leg off.

Shawn nudged me. I did the talking anytime it had to do with grownups, but for some reason, I was frozen in my tracks.

"What do you want?" The guy huffed, talking fast like he had people waiting. "I got something on the stove."

Shawn sniffed the air. "He's cooking bacon," he whispered from behind me. "Bacon's number two on my top ten."

Shawn had a top-ten food list that he was always updating. I had memorized the most recent one:

1) cheez-whirlz
2) bacon
3) watermelon
4) dill pickles
5) caramel popcorn
6) turkey drumsticks
7) onion rings
8) corn on the cob
9) deer jerky
10) marshmallow chicks

I choked the words out. "We were just wondering about those puppies . . . if we could see them and stuff."

The guy looked us over. Wiped his hands on his jeans and ran his tongue over his two front teeth, making this smacking noise. I've got this thing about teeth. I always check them out—I can't help it. This guy's teeth weren't bad, just kind of crooked.

"You have the money?" the guy said, doubtful.

I shook my head and turned to walk back down the porch steps. Shawn grabbed my arm hard and shoved me in front of the guy.

"Tell him about your birthday," he whispered. "About how your folks always give you a ton of money and buy you whatever you ask for . . ."

I dug my elbow into Shawn's side while the guy tapped the ashes from his cigarette onto the mailbox lid next to the door.

"I'm not saying that," I whispered back.

So then Shawn took over, his chin hitting my shoulder as he talked.

"See, it's like this. Russell here has a birthday coming up, and his folks always blow a bunch of money on it. Last year, man, what all did they get you, Russ?" Shawn tipped his head to one side and rolled his eyes up like he was thinking hard.

I had nothing for him. "I . . . can't remember."

Shawn kept up. "They got him a new game system and a big-screen TV and a go-cart and one of those spy watches with a little video camera in it . . ." Shawn trailed off as his mind turned to food again. "Oh yeah, and they got him a box—no, a whole case—of those chocolate Easter eggs that are kind of like real eggs, with a yellow yolk and everything, but they're chocolate. You like those?"

The guy frowned. "Hate 'em." He coughed into the crook of his arm, which was the first time I ever saw someone do that, even though it's what the nurse at school was always telling us to do.

Just then I heard a cell phone ring. As the guy fished the phone out of the pocket of his jeans, he propped the door open with his back and said, "They're in the basement. Don't touch them, and make it quick." Then he stepped onto the porch and took the call while Shawn and I ducked inside.

It was dark in that house. Every shade was

pulled. My eyes started to adjust as I led the way through what I guessed was the living room. Where was the basement door? Shawn opened the bathroom door and closed it quick in case the guy came back inside and thought we were snooping. I spotted another door toward the back of the kitchen.

Shawn and I picked our way through the kitchen, past the bacon that was now smoking in a pan filled with grease. I knew that if Shawn thought no one was looking, he would have grabbed a piece. But I also knew he was thinking the same thing I was. What if this guy was some sort of mass murderer? Sure, the puppies were in the basement. Wouldn't that be the perfect trick to lure kids in before he put the stranglehold on them? I'd never been too thrilled about basements, anyway. Call me chicken, but there was just something freaky about going up or down basement stairs that got me every time. All I can think about is a pair of bony hands clawing around my ankles and pulling me down. That's why I avoid basements as much as possible.

But this was about puppies. Rottweiler puppies. Even though the barking was louder and even more murderous sounding than before, I turned the doorknob leading to the basement just as I heard the guy come back in off the porch. We headed down three steps to a junky landing where there was a door that opened to the backyard. Then we continued down the rest of the stairs. I heard the guy swearing at his burned bacon, like it was the bacon's fault for being left on the stove. I also heard the basement door slam.

The only light we had was coming in from the smudgy basement windows. It was just enough for us to see that every inch of the steps was covered with dirty clothes—ripped-up jeans, work shirts with their sleeves cut off, wads of black socks, brown towels, and an orange blanket with oil stains. It was Mount Washmore and we were at the peak.

"I'm going to break my neck on these stairs," Shawn said.

I started clearing a path with my foot, kicking clothes from the center of the steps to the basement floor below. Everything smelled damp.

"It'll be all right. Come on," I said.

Shawn grabbed the back of my T-shirt. "If this guy sells us a puppy, he better go buy some light bulbs."

I could hear the puppies—grunting and chuffing around, kicking up the smell of rotten newspapers. I heard panting coming from the shadows in the corner, and I figured out quick that there was something else there that was definitely not a puppy.

I stopped on the last step. Shawn plastered himself behind me.

"Think we should just . . . feel around?" Shawn said.

I nodded. I stuck out my hands, crouched down low, and walked off the step. So did Shawn. Slowly we tiptoed toward the corner, and as we did, there was growling. Snarling. It had to be the puppies' mama.

I held my breath.

It was too late to go back up the steps. My mind raced. Bacon-eating mass murderer upstairs, kid-eating mama rottweiler downstairs. We were dead either way.

A bit more light streamed in from the basement window. Mama came closer to us. Now I could easily make out her white teeth. Her head was as big as a Halloween pumpkin—at least the smallish ones they sell at the dollar store. I started rating my body parts in order of importance. A chunk of leg wouldn't be that bad, but if she bit off my hand, that would be a whole different deal. I kind of liked my face, too. Except for my front teeth. Maybe my left elbow would have been okay, since it was always getting dislocated.

"Don't look her in the eye," Shawn whispered. "Dogs take that as a challenge."

Every once in a while Shawn said something that made sense. So I looked at the ceiling, and I noticed that the mass murderer had a cool bow-and-arrow set hanging from one of the beams. Then I realized that my neck was extended—a perfect target for Mama. Time stood still.

I got an idea.

I changed my voice to be the happiest, sappiest anyone's ever heard, with a touch of Sunday school puppet lady thrown in, too. "Oh, sweet little baby, how's Papa's big girlie girl? Such a cutey-patooty you are, yes you are . . ."

A deeper growl answered me.

"Who says 'cutey-patooty'?" Shawn hissed. "Even a dog knows how dorky that sounds."

"Got something better?" I realized I had to go to the bathroom. It happened sometimes when there was an emergency.

"Let's back up," said Shawn. "Keep looking at the ceiling."

"Watch your neck," I whispered.

We took a step backwards, a big mistake. Shawn stumbled and fell over an old sleeping bag we had kicked off the steps. I landed directly on him. Mama had her chance. She pounced, and suddenly it was a Russell sandwich. Shawn on the bottom, me face-up in the middle, and four giant rottweiler paws on top of me.

Chapter Three

I felt Shawn wiggle his hand into his pocket. He pulled out a fistful of cheez-whirlz.

I gritted my teeth. "You cannot be thinking of food now!"

Shawn's voice was squeaky under the weight. "Not . . . for . . . me."

With a twist of his wrist, Shawn scattered the cheez-whirlz across the floor. Mama turned her head. Food. She took a paw off my chest and bent to eat one. The trail of orange cheez-whirlz stretched to the corner where the puppies were curled up. One of them raised its sleepy head and looked at me. Its shiny black nose and rusty eyebrows were so cute I forgot for a second what was happening—then remembered with a jolt what was on top of me. Another paw stepped off. Shawn dug his chin into my shoulder to get my attention, like I hadn't noticed.

"It . . . worked," he said.

Mama was off, but there were only five cheezwhirlz left for her to find. That gave us exactly one second to stand and run up the basement stairs before she turned her attention from her appetizer to her dinner—which was us.

We had no other choice.

"RUN!" I shouted. We both bolted to our feet, but Shawn was first to scale the steps, three at once. I was right behind him as he crashed into the basement door and swung it open just in time. But Mama had bounded up the stairs after us. I was almost through the door when I felt it. Mama had the back of my too-big T-shirt in her mouth. I lunged through the doorway anyway. One more chomp meant that Mama was going to be taking a chunk out of my back, a body part I forgot to rate. Suddenly it was real important.

"Slam the door! Slam it!" I yelled to Shawn.

Shawn slammed it hard with all his weight. Mama was on the other side, with most of my T-shirt still in her mouth. My collar stretched tight, digging into my neck. The door rattled and shook each time she jumped against it. I was tethered by my T-shirt.

"I think I'm having a heart attack," Shawn said.

Ever since Shawn saw a commercial about what to do if you're having a heart attack, he always thought he was having one. "Feel." He grabbed my hand and slapped it on his chest.

I yanked my hand away. "I can't tell if you're having a heart attack! Besides, what could I do if you were? I'm stuck to this door!"

Just then I noticed the guy, leaning against the

kitchen counter, arms crossed. He had a weird smile on his face, like we were amusing him. I bet if Uncle Cory were here, he would have hauled off and punched him.

Popping a piece of bacon in his mouth, the guy opened a kitchen drawer by the sink. He pulled out a knife. A knife long enough to stab a skinny kid through, from one side to the other.

"Hey, whatcha got that for?" Shawn asked, his voice going high like it always did when he was freaking out.

The guy walked toward us fast. He raised the knife in the air, killer-style. I froze. Shawn crouched in fight position—of the two of us, he was more likely to win in any battle. He also had a good chance to run and leave me behind, but I knew he wouldn't.

"Put it down!" Shawn yelled at the guy, but the guy raised the knife higher. He stepped toward us, grabbed my shoulder, and brought the knife down against . . . the back of my T-shirt. He sawed back and forth a few times, and I was released from the door.

He tossed the knife on the kitchen table. Didn't miss a beat.

"Find one you like?" he asked.

Shawn acted cool, like he wasn't having a heart attack a minute before.

"One what?"

The guy sighed, getting annoyed again. He rubbed his sideburns fast, like he was shining them.

"The puppies," he said.

"Yeah. There were a couple we had our eyes on. Right, Russell?" Shawn said.

I nodded. Of course we had barely seen them, since we were kind of busy staying alive.

"Bring me some money, and I'll save one for you."

I could finally talk. "How much for the first payment?" I asked.

"Ahhh . . . ten bucks."

Shawn shrugged and gave a smirk. "Is that all?"

The guy called his bluff. "Okay, twenty, then."

"Oh, ten is just fine." Shawn stuck out his hand, businesslike.

"My name's Shawn Timmerman, and this is Russell Woods," he said.

The guy shook Shawn's hand. "Nick," he said. He didn't tell us his last name. "Come back when you've got the first payment—not before."

I was suddenly aware that the back half of my shirt was missing, and the neck was so bagged out it could slip down my shoulder. I hitched and tucked as best I could, but it was no use.

Just then Mama jumped at the basement door again. The doorknob rattled. She wasn't giving up. My mind flashed forward to us going back down into the zone of death.

Nick scowled and pounded hard on the door a couple times.

"PRINCESS—knock it off!"

Princess knocked it off. She gave a whine, and

then all we heard was panting. Nick turned back to Shawn and me.

"I'll tie her out back next time you come, so you can get downstairs. No use wrecking another T-shirt," he said, motioning us toward the front door with his head.

Shawn's lips were in a tight line, holding back a smile. He'd heard it, too. "Deal," he said.

Shawn and I headed for the door. I felt a laugh rising up, and because I had to go to the bathroom so bad, I knew if I let that laugh spill, it was over. Chopped T-shirt *and* wet pants.

Shawn stumbled onto the porch, weak from the effort of holding back. We hopped onto the bike, this time Shawn pedaling and me behind. We barely made it around the corner to an empty lot and I ditched the bike. I ran behind a tree to quickly take care of the emergency while Shawn crumpled into a heap in a full-blown laughing frenzy.

Then I joined him. "He . . . named . . . that . . . dog . . . PRINCESS!"

Chapter Four

It was time to cook up a plan to get money. We tried out ideas on the walk to school.

"Your mom owe you anything right now?" I asked Shawn. Shawn's mom sometimes borrowed change to buy gas to get to Des Moines, where she cleaned rooms at a fancy hotel. Shawn's dad never borrowed money, because he never went any-where. He had something wrong with his lungs and hadn't worked in a long time. Mostly he cooked, yelled after Shawn's five older brothers, and tried to stay close to the fan or air conditioner. He said it helped him breathe.

"Nah, my mom just paid me back," Shawn said. "With that money, I bought a couple bags of cheez-whirlz and that candy brain from the DX."

"Gross," I said. Shawn loved disgusting candy, and at the DX they had it all. Candy eyeballs, candy boogers, candy brains.

I tried again. "How about your brothers?"

Shawn shook his head. "No way. They're just as broke as we are. Oh, wait . . . Travis has a job, but his car only runs in reverse, so most of his money's going to fixing it."

Shawn looked at me, hopeful. "Your uncle Cory have any cash?"

"Maybe—but not any that he'd lend me for a dog."

Shawn picked up a stick and swatted at weeds as we walked.

"Man, why does he hate dogs so much?"

I remembered my dad's stories. They always

started with "my crazy little brother Cory . . ." and once he'd start, he'd talk fast and look over my head, like if he thought about it for a second, he'd change his mind and not finish, especially when the story involved Uncle Cory picking locks, breaking in, and getting away with stuff. I always wondered if there was some little part of him that was proud of the bad stuff Uncle Cory did. The dog-hating stories were more neutral. For those, he'd look me in the eyes at least.

"He got bit twice," I told Shawn. "Once by his neighbor's schnauzer and another time at the salvage yard when one of the German shepherds guarding the place chomped his ankle. Oh, and his buddy's Great Dane lifted his leg and peed inside his new motorcycle boots."

Shawn laughed. "That's better than biting, I guess."

At school, Shawn told me to meet him at the usual time before he headed to sixth grade homeroom with Mr. Delaney. I had Miss Chandler for homeroom. Both were brand-new teachers, nervous and dressed nice. At William Harrison Middle School, teachers didn't stick around for long . . . sometimes not even the whole year. Maybe it was because of who the school was named after. William Harrison was a guy who didn't stick around for long, either. He got sworn in as the ninth president and a month later croaked from pneumonia.

When William Harrison Middle School was on the news because of a school supply drive, Mr. Mackie, the principal, said in a drippy voice that we were having a drive because so many of the students at our school were "under-resourced." I thought that sounded like just another way to say "poor," and it bugged me, maybe because I was one of the kids standing in line on the first day of school, waiting for my free pencils and folders.

At the beginning of the year, Shawn and I timed out when we would go to the bathroom—9:37 a.m., 11:17 a.m., 1:10 p.m., and 2:50 p.m. Any more often than that, and teachers got suspicious and sent you to the nurse with an embarrassing note. Any longer than five minutes away, and they thought maybe you were the kid who wadded up balls of toilet paper, soaked them with water, and pitched them up at the bathroom ceiling.

At the first bathroom break, we tried out more moneymaking ideas, starting with collecting pop cans.

I figured out the math.

"We'd need to pick up a hundred cans to get ten dollars."

"How many do you usually find in a day?" Shawn asked.

"Four or five. Once, I found six."

"So, how long would it take to find a hundred?" Shawn ran the water so it looked like he was washing his hands, in case a teacher walked past.

"Over a month, and that's just for the first payment. By then the puppies might be gone."

At the second bathroom break Shawn said that maybe baby-sitting would work. His cousin baby-sat for a rich family and got twenty dollars for two hours, and all she did was watch the kids sleep.

"She got to eat whatever she wanted, too, and they had chocolate frosting in a can and graham crackers. So the last time she went, she made frosting sandwiches and—"

I interrupted, since we didn't have much time. "How old is your cousin?" I asked, flushing the toilet.

"Fifteen, I think," Shawn said. "But if we did it together, and we're eleven, then that would be like a . . . twenty-two-year-old. Right?"

I looked at Shawn. "Have you ever seen those babysitter books girls read?"

Shawn's face brightened, like I was going along with his baby-sitting plan. "Yeah, I've seen them. Are you going to read them so we'll know what we're doing when some mom calls us to watch her kid?"

"Remember the covers of those books? That's what parents think a babysitter should look like. A girl with a ponytail, white teeth, and clothes that aren't wrinkly. Maybe she's got a bike with a basket filled with books she's going to read to their kid . . . That's not us, Shawn."

Shawn had worn the same shirt for three days—a wolf howling at the moon. One of his shoes didn't have any laces, and his jeans had a hole in the knee that he'd covered with duct tape. All the clothes he owned were hand-me-downs from his brothers, and by the time they got to him, they were one stop from the garbage can.

My clothes weren't much better. When my dad got arrested, I had no time to pack up my stuff. It was grab and go. I used two garbage bags. In one I stuffed five T-shirts, two pairs of jeans, a brown Rufus AutoBody hooded sweatshirt, and some green football pants in case I ever went out for football.

In the other bag I packed a photo of my mom in a frame from the dollar store and a leather key chain with a cross on it that I found under the picnic table at the park. I also packed four comic books and a feather pillow from my mom's side of the bed that smelled nice but leaked feathers, especially if you threw it at someone.

Uncle Cory filled in the rest from the thrift store, since he didn't have money for new clothes. My thrift store T-shirts advertised stuff that other kids did—a soccer tournament in 2004, band camp, a trip to Disney World. My haircuts came from the hair-cutting college—on the two-for-one days. Uncle Cory got his long hair trimmed, and I got a buzzcut. His looked fine, but mine always grew out straight and spiky from my head, like a blond Chia pet.

Shawn was quiet, sitting on the floor in the farthest corner of the bathroom, behind the garbage can—our usual spot. He tucked his shoe that didn't have a lace under one leg like he was embarrassed all of a sudden.

"Whatever. So we need another idea," he finally said. "I have to eat lunch fast today, and then

Mr. Delaney's helping me with math. I'll meet you back here at ten after one. This time, you come up with something."

At 1:10, I brought a list along with me that had both the ideas and what was wrong with each idea. Shawn hit the button on the hand dryer as he read.

Lawn Mowing: Don't have a lawn mower
Sell Stuff: Don't have stuff
Get a Real Job: Not old enough
Bake Sale: Don't know how to bake. No oven in the camper

"Well, this is a dumb list," Shawn remarked.

"Like baby-sitting was any better. How many rich parents with little kids do you know, anyway?"

"A lot more than you," Shawn said. "I know lots of people that you don't even know I know."

I didn't believe him for a second. "Right. Name one."

Just then Mr. Delaney stuck his head in the bathroom door. "Gentlemen, keep moving. Back to class."

At 2:50 I thought about not going to the bathroom, since Shawn said my list was dumb. But then I thought about those puppies—those rottweiler puppies with their round bellies, wet noses, and orange eyebrows. They couldn't help that they had a deranged mother any more than I could help that my dad was in prison.

I met Shawn in the bathroom. Head down, his forehead on his knees.

"Got anything?" Shawn said.

"No—do you?" I sat down next to him. A third-grader who got bused from the elementary to William Harrison for math because he was so smart came in to use the bathroom. I told him it was closed.

"How come?" he asked.

Shawn took over. "Stuff shoots out of the toilet if you flush it."

The third-grader stood there, his mouth open.

"In fact, they asked me and Russ to guard the bathroom because the force from the toilet is so strong it shot some kid right up there." Shawn scoped out the ceiling and pointed to a missing tile. "See, that's where he hit."

The third-grader's face turned red.

"Does—the first-floor bathroom work?" he stammered.

"Oh, that one works fine," Shawn said.

After school, Shawn had detention for not turning in his language arts homework. Maybe because Shawn wasn't around, Terry Grundel knocked me in the back with his trombone case for no reason, even though he acted like he was just getting stuff out of his locker.

Terry was big and brainy and had won over every teacher because he got good grades and had friends. But they didn't see his rotten side.

He was the kid who aimed for my head in every game that involved a ball.

He was the kid who told me so many times that honestly, Jasmine Weyer liked me, she really did, that I started believing it a little bit. But then I saw Jasmine Weyer laughing because Terry pointed out all the warts I had on my knuckles.

He was the kid who, when I was standing in front of the line, unzipped my backpack without me knowing it, showing everyone the dirty pop cans I'd collected.

And he was the kid who was real nice to me one time at recess and got me to tell him about my dad and what he got busted for. Then he gave a speech at the Character Counts assembly and used enough details so that everyone knew he was talking about my dad and how he didn't have good character. But he didn't use my dad's name, so he wouldn't get into trouble.

A big rottweiler would put a stop to someone like Terry Grundel. One charge, one good bite, and that'd be the end. I walked home alone, without even stopping at the DX for a blue raspberry, since there weren't enough cans that morning.

At home, Uncle Cory's motorcycle was gone, so I dug around for a house key in the bottom of an old boot by the door and let myself in for something to eat. Every time I went into Uncle Cory's house, I got this pang that made me wonder . . . Why *did* I sleep in the camper? The house was a lot like Nick's, shabby and worn out, but with something different, too. My school picture was taped on the fridge. Too bad I looked like a dork. When I flipped his calendar to March, I saw the date of my birthday circled.

And in his cupboard, there was the kind of macaroni and cheese where the macaroni is shaped like little race cars. It had to be for me.

Uncle Cory was ten years younger than my dad . . . out of high school five years. How could a guy that age be all about settling down and raising me? In my mind, I decided he was doing it because I didn't have anybody else. He was decent enough not to let them put me in a youth shelter, but I didn't trust it went beyond that. For now, being decent had to be good enough.

I pulled out the macaroni and cheese and found a pot to start the water boiling. When my dinner finished cooking, I grabbed a spoon, sat down at the kitchen table, and ate right out of the pot, with the macaroni and cheese box in front of me for entertainment. I was secretly pleased to chase those cheesy race cars around with my spoon, and the smiling little kid they had on the front of the box looked like he thought it was cool, too.

But with every bite my mind kept nudging around the thing that was really bugging me— those puppies, and how all we needed was ten bucks to get one set aside for us.

Ten dollars. That was it.

For the first time in my life I thought about doing something I swore I'd never do . . .

Follow in my dad's footsteps and . . .

steal the money.

Chapter Five

That night, the wind rocked the camper, and the battery in my flashlight stopped working, so I couldn't even read. A pine branch scraped against the camper canvas, sounding like the fingernails of something creepy. I checked the chair propped up under the door and wadded up my mom's pillow, pulling it close. I pretended that the lump of pillow was a mean old dog with its heart set on protecting me. I even growled, like a dog would if he heard what I was hearing.

I huddled there, thinking that if I had a mom who was alive, she'd stay awake until I fell asleep, working out a crossword puzzle or something. Maybe she'd even stay up later in case I had a nightmare or started coughing. If I had a dad around, he'd go check things out, with no shirt or shoes on and a baseball bat in his hand. That was the way it was supposed to be . . . kids with parents, or at least with someone who watched out for them. For now, it was me alone, with a pillow dog.

Since there was no one to talk to, I decided to talk to God and tell Him about the puppies and the money and how I really hated Terry Grundel. I was going to leave out the stealing part, but I changed my mind. I figured there were people right then telling Him about a lot worse things they actually did, not just thought of doing. Afterward I just lay there, deciding I wasn't going to steal the money and wondering if God was going to send some kind of nice message to me. It was quiet, but then He answered me with a huge gust of wind that ripped open the door of the camper. The chair clattered to the ground. My heart felt like it was going to pop.

One time in Sunday school the teacher said, "God is a MYSTERY. Can you all say MYSTERY?" As if we were too stupid to say the word, she said it real slow, and her eyes got all wide. I went along with it. I didn't get it at the time, but when you talk to God about wanting a dog so bad you feel like you're going to throw up, and then God rips open your camper door with a big gust of wind when the latch is only a little bit loose—and there's a chair under it—maybe this was the kind of mystery she was talking about.

I shut the camper door, hooked the chair back under the handle, and listened to the wind howl. I practiced my challenge words in spelling. Terry and I were the only ones in our class who were in challenge spelling, and right now, he had a better score. If I beat him, though, he wouldn't just hit me with his trombone case, he'd squish me into it. I didn't get a chance to practice long, because I heard some-one shout my name.

"Russell!"

I lay perfectly still, not breathing. It sounded like Shawn, but I couldn't be sure.

"Russell!" The voice was louder.

The camper door rattled, and I knew that with one big yank, anyone or anything could attack me.

My mind raced—I needed a weapon.

I grabbed the closest thing I could find in the dark, a fishing net that came with the camper. I crouched in fight position, ready to spring, like I'd seen Shawn do a hundred times. He said his mom told him that with all his older brothers, his hands were in fists when he was born for a good reason. I raised my fists close to my face. My heart thudded. I wondered if that was one of those heart attack warning signs. It probably was.

The camper door was pulled hard. Once, twice, three times, and it popped open. The chair crashed to the floor again.

I screamed, threw the fishing net at the intruder, and jumped under the covers.

"Russell—it's me!" the voice said. As the alley light shone in the camper door, Shawn came into focus. He pulled off the net. "Did you think a killer fish was coming for you?" He had something in his hand. The pooper-scooper.

I shut the door. Shawn sat on the bench and grabbed a blanket for his skinny shoulders. He never wore a coat. I didn't know if he even had one.

"What are you doing here? And why'd you bring that?" I said, pointing to the pooper-scooper and taking a seat, too.

Shawn squeezed the handle, and it opened and shut. He stared at it like it was alive.

Then he got right in my face and said in a serious voice, "I've got a plan, and it couldn't wait until tomorrow—so I rode my bike over to tell you."

I leaned in close, as the wind picked up. Shawn wasn't serious very often. "What is it?"

"Ready for this one?"

I nodded.

"We scoop poop for people's dogs. For every one we scoop, we charge the owners ten cents. Big dogs cost double—twenty cents. Gigantic dogs cost a quarter."

I thought for a while. Shawn had even gotten the math right. "You think people will pay us to scoop up after their dogs?"

"Maybe not around here, but somewhere else they might."

Ideas started to spin in my head. I read a book once about a kid who had a dog-washing business, and he printed up flyers and took them to all of his neighbors, and his business had a name and everything. And that kid made enough money to buy a brand-new bike from a store.

"We'll need flyers," I said.

"And bags for the . . . doo-doo," Shawn said.

"We're not calling it doo-doo, are we?"

Shawn laughed. "Nah, let's call it what it is."

"We have to have a business name . . . something official."

"How about the Doo-doo Dudes?" Shawn said.

"Will you stop with the doo-doo?"

"Okay, how about the Super Dooper Pooper Scoopers?"

"Super Dooper is kind of corny. No one says that."

"Maybe not, but it sounds cool when you say the whole thing together—Super Dooper Pooper Scoopers."

"It's long. If we did the initials, it would be SDPS."

"I'll never remember that," Shawn said. "How about just PS?"

"That's good . . . then sometimes a business will have the person's name in it—like, uh, Rufus AutoBody. Rufus is a real guy."

"So like Shawn and Russell's PS Business? That's kind of long, too."

We sat there racking our brains.

"I've got it!" Shawn said. "We're like brothers, and we'll be poop scooping. What if we called it the PS Brothers?"

The wind died down. I reached over to give Shawn a high-five. Since it was kind of dark, I smacked his face by accident. There was something real great about the PS Brothers. It fit us.

"Okay, so we're going to start work tomorrow, right?" Shawn said. "How long do you think it will take to get ten bucks?"

"I don't know. It'll depend on the size of the dogs. But let's say we hit the jackpot and scoop all huge dogs tomorrow at twenty-five cents per scoop. It's only forty scoops all together."

"Man, that's not bad," Shawn said.

"Bring your pooper-scooper with you in the morning, and we'll go find some business after school, okay? Oh . . . do you have any plastic bags?"

Shawn threw the blanket off his shoulders and opened the camper door. "We've got a lot of them at home. I'll bring some along," he said as we both stepped outside.

Up and down the street, the houses were dark. The wind had blown the cloud cover away, and the stars were shining. Shawn hopped on his bike, one hand on the handlebars and the other on the pooper-scooper.

"Farewell, my brother," he said. "If I don't come to school tomorrow, I've been abducted by aliens and I'm riding around in that UFO we thought we saw last year."

"Make sure you put up a good fight," I said. I gave him a wave, went back into the camper, and climbed into bed, suddenly feeling as close to hopeful as I ever had. I had a business . . . a brother . . . and someday I would have a dog.

Chapter Six

The next day at school, time moved backwards. We did the state tests where you had to fill in the little ovals with a number two pencil. The test had questions like how far was it between towns Jot and Tab. I measured the distance and tried to get the answer right, but inside I was thinking, Whoever heard of towns named Jot and Tab?

I kept going but got distracted again when it came to the math story problems. One had a kid buying supplies to build a lemonade stand. The supplies cost $73.00. What kid had $73.00 in his pocket? Another story problem had two girls earning $50.00 for raking Mrs. Brown's leaves. *Fifty dollars?* And the last one really bugged me. This boy bought a slice of pizza at the ballpark for $6.75. You could get two corn dogs for a buck at the DX. For $6.75 you could get thirteen and a half corn dogs, and you'd be full for a week.

The worst thing about state testing days was not getting to talk to Shawn until lunch or right after, since the bathroom breaks were taken a whole class at a time. We had to form two lines outside the boys' and girls' restrooms, and four kids would go in at once.

At lunch Shawn was across the room, and before I could reach him, it got so noisy that Mr. Delaney shut off the lights. "Silence for the rest of the lunch period," he said.

The lunch lady didn't have to be quiet. She yelled that anyone who wanted to could have seconds on something called hamburger hot dish. There would be at least two kids in line—Shawn and me. We always got seconds, even if it was hamburger hot dish. If the meal included something in a package, like crackers, Shawn stuffed them in his pocket for later. When you had a mess of brothers, you had to think ahead.

Shawn held out his tray, and the lunch lady plopped down a rounded tan lump of hamburger and Tater Tots mushed together. I held out my own tray.

While eating round two, I looked out the cafeteria window and saw that it had started to rain. Mr. Delaney noticed, too, and made an announcement that the fifteen-minute break we got after lunch would be in our homerooms rather than outside.

"Three more hours," Shawn whispered, shuffling into line with his class. "Meet me at the bike rack."

"Got it," I said.

Nothing was worse than inside recess without Shawn. I grabbed a book from my desk while everyone else got out a game or drew on the chalkboard or sat in little groups. I didn't have a little group. I propped my book in front of me like I was reading, but I was working on our business flyers so they'd be ready after school. Terry Grundel walked past with a stack of board games. One knocked me hard on the side of my face.

Terry faked it. "Oh, sorry about that, Russell," he said. "Did you want to play checkers?"

I lowered my head behind my book, covering the flyers with my arms.

We took tests all afternoon, and by the end of the day, my head hurt. Miss Chandler had a wrinkled look on her face, like she was fixing to cry.

"Our school," she had gulped that morning, "is in need of improvement, and better test scores will show we're improving, boys and girls."

I glanced over at this kid named Reginald Paltry and saw that he had made designs with his little ovals. No wonder he was always done first.

Terry finished close behind, but I was pretty sure his answers were right. Even with the test, he had plenty of time to kick my desk and blow his hamburger hot dish breath on me while I worked.

When the final bell rang, I was out the door. I took the back stairwell to avoid Terry and headed to the bike rack. Shawn was there. He had already retrieved the pooper-scooper from its new hiding place under the school Dumpster.

"Hop on," he said as he pounded the seat of his bike. I straddled the seat and threw my backpack over my shoulder. We beat the buses out of the parking lot and rode down the street. Luckily, the rain had stopped and the puddles had dried up.

"Where do we go?" Shawn asked.

"I've been thinking about that," I said. "We're

going to have to experiment. We should try some rich houses by the park. Then let's go over by the bowling alley, where the houses aren't that big, and then let's try some in our neighborhood."

"So over by the park first?"

"Yep. Remember that kid who came to school for three days and then his parents pulled him out? He lives in a huge house over there."

We rode down thirteen blocks, up and down sidewalks, in and out of alleys—every shortcut we could think of.

The yards began to stretch out, not a scrap of litter or cigarette butt or oil stain anywhere.

"I don't know, Russ," Shawn said. "These people have too much money to let a dog poop in their yard."

But then I saw it as we pedaled past a brick house with a white poodle inside the fence. A small brown lump in the grass. I squinted. Another lump in the corner. Not exactly the big money, at ten cents a scoop, but still, a place to start.

"Shawn—look! Our first customer!"

We jumped off the bike, and Shawn let it fall to the ground. We ran to the front door of the house, and I ripped a flyer out of my backpack so we were ready.

I rang the doorbell. "I'll do the talking."

An old guy in a blue bathrobe answered the door and took a confused look at us. "I gave at the office," he said, and began to close the door. Shawn shoved me so I was practically chest to belly with the guy.

"Sir, I noticed that you have a dog in your yard, and because it's a dog, it poops outside, and someone needs to clean that up. Well, we're the PS Brothers, and your dog and his business is our business. We'll clean up after your dog, for a small charge, of course."

I shoved a flyer into the old guy's wrinkly hand.

"You mean to tell me that you'll pick up after my dog for ten cents a . . . a—"

"Poop? Yes, sir. That's right," I replied.

Shawn bounced his head up and down like a basketball. He held up one of the plastic grocery store bags he had brought from home. "We come prepared."

The guy scratched his head. "Well, that's quite a deal. Ah, go ahead. See how many you can find back there—maybe there's a few."

Shawn and I raced to the guy's backyard. At first the white poodle in her little pink collar yapped at us, but when I scratched behind her ears, she rolled over for a belly rub.

Then Shawn and I started hunting for poops like they were Easter eggs.

"Found one!" Shawn yelled.

"Here's another!"

"One in the corner!"

Shawn was the spotter, and I was the scooper . . . brotherly, I thought. The old guy came out on his patio to watch, and when we were done, we showed him the bag.

"There are thirteen poops. Do you want us to count them for you? 'Cause that's a service we're offering all our customers," I said.

The guy shook his head, and he had a hint of a smile on his face. "No need to count them—I believe you. In fact, come back next week if you want. I'm sure there'll be more."

After getting paid our $1.30 and thanking our first customer, we rode over by the bowling alley and scanned that neighborhood. There were smaller houses, swing sets in the backyards, and older cars in the driveways.

At a two-story house with lots of Halloween decorations on the porch, we saw a dog chain snaked on the grass. There were muddy paw prints on the steps, and they looked big. This one could be a moneymaker.

A teenager answered the door and told us that cleaning up after the dog was his job, but if we only charged twenty cents a scoop, he'd pay us to do it for him.

When we got to the backyard, we saw the disaster. Shawn was so excited he did a careful handstand in the only clean part of the yard.

"This might do it! If we scoop this whole yard and add that to the dollar thirty, we'll probably have ten dollars!" Shawn said.

We got to work. This time I did the spotting and counting, and Shawn did the scooping.

Because the dog was humongous, my job wasn't too hard. From all the dog books I had read, I figured it was half Newfoundland and half elephant. I could see the black, furry giant inside the patio door, first barking, then licking the door glass with a big, drooly tongue, then flopping down for a snooze.

It took us time to clean that yard. My stomach growled, and I noticed that the sun was just starting to set. Two of our bags were full, and finally the yard was done. We had scooped forty-two poops. I added them up quick.

"That's eight dollars and forty cents!" I told Shawn.

Shawn's voice went high as he started to freak out.

"Do you think he'll pay? What if he doesn't believe there were so many? Are we going to have to dump them out and count them again?"

We knocked on the patio door, and the teenage kid answered it. This time he had a mixing bowl filled with cereal and about half a gallon of milk poured on it.

"We scooped forty-two. That will be eight forty." I stuck out my hand, palm up. When it came to money, I had bold bones.

The teenager glanced at the bulging bags on his steps and made a grossed-out face. He set his cereal down and pulled a ten-dollar bill from his jeans. As he gave it to us, his dog crowded through the door. Shawn knelt down and petted his head. The dog planted a sloppy kiss across his cheek.

"Keep the change," the kid said. Then he patted his leg and called his dog back in.

I held the ten dollars in my hand, not sure of what had just happened. Our first day! Our first tip! Shawn slapped me on the back, laughing.

"We got it! Oh, man, Russell, we did it!"

I grabbed him by the shoulders, and we danced around in the teenage kid's yard like a couple of weirdoes.

Then I shouted, "Let's ride to Nick's and choose our puppy!"

Chapter Seven

...

On the way to Nick's, we stopped and bought two corn dogs at the DX. The lady behind the counter let us have ice water for free. We gulped down our supper and made it to Nick's in record time.

Shawn knocked on the door, but there was no answer. Princess barked from the basement. "Maybe he's down there with her and can't hear us."

I elbowed my way through a bush and crouched down to look in the basement window, wiping the grime and cobwebs away with the bottom of my T-shirt. No Nick, but Princess heard me and jumped at the wall where the window was.

"I'll bet he's out back," Shawn said. "His car is here, so he's got to be around."

There were three kennels in the backyard, attached to each other under a rusty tin roof. Each kennel had its own gate. One kennel had a brindle-colored pit bull in it, but the other two were empty. I usually pet every dog I meet, if they act like they want me to, but this one was growling and barking, so I held back. Shawn tossed it a cheez-whirlz, but he wasn't crazy enough to pet it, either.

Next to the kennels was a gray garage, which definitely leaned to one side. If someone like Uncle Cory gave it a shove, it would probably fall right over. All the garage windows were boarded over, but the side entrance door was brand-new, with the price sticker still on it. Heavy steel, with a peephole that someone could look out of from the inside, but the outside guy couldn't look in. I heard hammering, and there was a trail of hay leading up to the door. Maybe Nick had a horse?

We pounded on the door. The hammering stopped.

"Nick! It's us—Russell and Shawn!"

After a while Nick opened the door, and then shut it behind him fast, like he didn't want us to see the Christmas presents he bought for us.

I pulled the ten dollars from my pocket. "Here it is . . . that money you wanted before we could pick out a puppy."

Nick grabbed the money and looked around. He stamped out his half-smoked cigarette, and pulled the pack from his shirt pocket. He lit another one and took a fast draw.

"I'll take Princess outside so you can go down in the basement. Give me a minute, will ya?"

Nick stamped out his new cigarette, and we followed him to the back door of the house. Shawn hopped up and down, his arms wrapped around his chest, while Nick went inside. In a minute Nick came back out, with one hand gripped around Princess's thick collar, steering her toward the kennel. In his other hand he had a flashlight.

"Here, take this," he said, shoving the flashlight at me before Princess pulled him away.

"Let's go in," Shawn said, holding open the back door to the stair landing. I walked onto the landing and went up the three steps to open the kitchen door for more light. I handed Shawn the flashlight; then together we headed down the stairs and straight to the corner where the puppies whimpered and grunted.

Our eyes started to adjust. I grabbed a beat-up box with a bunch of chains in it and some long sticks with teeth marks. I dumped the box out on the basement floor.

"Let's put all the puppies in here and bring them upstairs to look at them."

We sat on the kitchen floor and crouched over that box of six puppies. They nosed around, eyes wide open, bellies low. Mostly black, with little orange eyebrows and a tannish mask. Shawn picked one up and put it next to his cheek. It struggled and wiggled and turned its head to bite Shawn's earlobe.

"This one's got a good bite."

I petted each one and put them all on my lap.

"We want a boy, right?"

Shawn looked at me like I was nuts for asking. He separated them out after turning them over for a peek. He put the four girls in an old laundry basket Nick had sitting in the kitchen, and he kept the two boy puppies in the box. That narrowed the choice.

One of the boy puppies curled up in a corner of the box and put his head on his paws to sleep. The other boy puppy did a little pounce on him and gnawed at the scruff of his neck.

I pictured Terry Grundel, Reginald Paltry, and this seventh grade kid named Montavious Smith. They were all kids who either wanted to beat me up or had a history of beating me up. Shawn had his own list, too. His even sort of had a girl. In fifth grade, Alyssa Clompton got a ring from a gum machine, bent up the little prongs, took out the jewel, then punched Shawn in the arm. It hurt bad, but he thought she did it because she was in love with him, like Deb, his library girlfriend. Alyssa wasn't really on the "kids who want to beat us up" list, but she was still a threat.

We watched that boy puppy keep on bothering the puppy trying to sleep—little growls coming out of him like he was tough. When he wasn't bugging the sleeping puppy, he was climbing and pouncing on us. A thought crossed my mind—I liked the sleepy puppy better. When I picked him up, he didn't struggle to get down. He just buried his warm head in my arm and made sweet noises, like I was the best thing that ever happened to him. But Shawn and I had agreed on getting a dog nobody would want to mess with—one that could protect us, not one all soft and cuddly that Terry Grundel could shut up with a swift kick. The growling puppy was giving us a sneak preview of what his personality was going to be like when he grew up. I had learned what "dominant" meant in the dog books I had read, and this puppy fit the description. Wasn't that what we wanted?

"How about him?" I asked.

"Yeah, he looks like a little fighter," Shawn said.

Nick came into the kitchen, and we held out the puppy we'd picked from the rest of the litter. Nick grabbed a green permanent marker from a green-bean can he had sitting on the windowsill, and he made a quick mark on the puppy's ear. The puppy chewed on Nick's hand.

"Get me the rest of the money, and he's yours. But bring it quick. I want these puppies out of here in two weeks."

When I heard that, the corn dog digesting in my stomach rolled around in a lurch. Two weeks? How much scooping would we have to do in order to get $190.00? I worked through the math in my head. If they were all small dogs, it would mean about 136 scoops a day, every day, for two whole weeks. Big dogs translated into 68 scoops a day. Were there even that many dogs in our whole town?

I dumped all of my worries on Shawn as he rode me back to the camper.

"Aw, we can do it, Russ," he said over his shoulder. "We've done way harder things before . . . like the time we built that tree house out of cardboard boxes and I fell through the floor and you caught my wrist like in the movies and saved my life."

I nodded. Shawn always remembered the important stuff.

"Or the time when your dad thought you broke his metal detector, and he was so mad we hid in the woods for two days with only my leftover school crackers and the plums from that old lady's tree? Russell, we do things that no other kids can do—not even if they tried their best."

I remembered another time. "How about when we wanted to play football, but we didn't have a real football, so you picked up that chunk of wood and tossed it to me, and it knocked out my tooth?"

Shawn dropped his head back and laughed. "Yeah, well, we've done stupid things before, too."

We made it back to the camper. It was late, and I still had to answer the comprehension questions in my social studies packet and finish my report on Booker T. Washington, using the alley light to see what I was doing. Even with that, and with our new deadline, Shawn had made me feel better.

"Don't forget the scooper . . . oh, and what about bags? You got enough?" I asked Shawn.

"I've got more at home, but if they run out, I found a barrel at the recycling center that's full of plastic bags. I wouldn't even feel bad about taking some, either, since we're putting them to good use and . . . you know, cleaning up the environment."

"Making it smell better, that's for sure."

"You're right," Shawn said, giving me a wave as he headed on his way back home.

Chapter Eight

 . . .

The next day, Terry Grundel knocked my binder out of my hand when we were on the way to science, and a flyer dropped to the ground. He grabbed it, read it, and started blabbing. It took exactly four minutes and forty-five seconds for the entire sixth grade at William Harrison Middle School to know how Shawn and I were employed.

By noon, we had heard it all. Shawn and I were . . .

sick,

freaks,

ghetto,

dweebs,

losers, who . . .

lived in a trash can,

Dumpster,

shack, with our

convicts,

bum relatives, and who . . .

scooped poop for a living and wore clothes that even the thrift store wouldn't give away. Not that some of the kids had room to talk when it came to clothes, but I still got nervous that they would focus on what I was wearing. Shawn and I had on matching socks. Uncle Cory had found a box full of striped socks behind the dollar store, next to the Dumpster, and he'd brought them home.

"Would you wear these, or are they . . . too weird?" he asked me.

I shrugged. "Yeah, I'd wear them."

I didn't want to make him feel bad for the offer. Shawn and I had divvied them up—twelve pairs each. They were good enough socks, but they were rainbow striped from the top down to the toes. The fact that Shawn and I matched added to their humiliation potential.

"Hey, we can start a fad," Shawn said. "I always wanted to start a fad. Pretty soon, kids will come banging on our door asking where we got these cool socks."

So far, that hadn't happened. I said a prayer that they wouldn't notice the socks, and I walked hunchy-like, which kept them covered up by my high-water jeans. It also made my knees hurt. It was a long day.

With the two-week deadline, the days became a blur of school and scooping. Every time we made ten dollars, we made a payment to Nick and he let us check on our puppy, who got bigger and bitier by the day. I kept track of our best customers in a spiral notebook, making sure we hit them up every few days. There was one house over by the bowling alley that had four golden retrievers and another in the rich neighborhood that boarded dogs when their owners went on vacation.

"Multiple dogs = fast money," I noted.

There was also the old lady who lived on the outskirts of town who gave Shawn and me baloney sandwiches on homemade bread when we were done scooping after her wirehaired terrier, Max. We saved her house for suppertime. Max always got part of my sandwich.

I wrote down our worst customers in the notebook, too, so we wouldn't accidentally go to their houses again. The owner who didn't tell us that her schnauzer had a bad case of diarrhea. The Chihuahua who had a thing for hiding under lawn furniture and then dashing out to attack ankles. The house where a lady asked us to walk her monstrous, leash-breaking mastiff, Bruno, after scooping, and she only gave us a quarter extra.

"I'm sure you had fun with my sweet boy Bruno, didn't you? Didn't you?" she said in a talking-to-a-baby voice.

"Never again," Shawn said as we both rubbed our shoulders from the dislocating Bruno had tried to do at his end of the leash.

"Deal," I said, and her name and address went into the notebook.

Of course, I also wrote down the tippers. There were some in every neighborhood—rich, poor, and in between.

Every time we went to Nick's with a payment, he was working in his garage or messing with the three pit bulls he now had. One day I asked him what he was doing in the garage, like we were old pals who had known each other for a hundred years.

"Are you fixing up a car in there? Or are you making a hangout?"

Nick turned quick, gave me a freezing, mean

look I hadn't seen before. It shut me down tight, but not Shawn.

"If you need some more of that hay, I got a cousin in Nebraska that kind of lives out in the country where there's a lot of hay. I'm sure he could bring some next time he visits."

Nick grabbed Shawn's arm, and Shawn jerked it out of his grip.

"What's your problem?" Shawn said, rubbing his arm.

"My problem is you two not minding your own business," Nick said. He spotted a corner of the ten-dollar bill sticking out of my shirt pocket and snatched it.

"You have four days to get the rest of the money," he said. "I've got people asking about that puppy, and I could easily sell it to one of them instead of waiting around for you two. Oh, and I'm keeping the first fifty as a deposit—that's mine whether you get the puppy or not."

With that, we started scooping before school . . . waking people up, making people mad, but we got some new customers. A black Lab by the Laundromat that ate crayons but could catch any Frisbee no matter how badly we threw it. A rust-colored dachshund named Dandy that pooped tootsie rolls and could shake with either paw.

We hung out at the dog park, too, as the official doggy janitors. Since the weather was good, there were usually eight to ten dogs running around in the enclosed park, sniffing each other, chasing tennis balls. We watched like hawks until one of them pooped. Then we presented our business plan to the person coming over to clean it up. Our customers at the dog park were the generous types, rounding up the payment for one or two poops to a dollar.

Sometimes it was hard to focus as we got to know the dogs we scooped for. What we really wanted to do was play with them, scratch behind their ears, rub their bellies, and throw them their

Frisbees. But we had only two days left, and forty dollars to go. It didn't matter what we wanted to do. This was all about what we needed to do.

That night, after scooping, we went over to Nick's and saw that the lights in the house were off, but cars lined the driveway. Back by the garage, the kennels were empty.

"What's going on?" Shawn asked. I squished my ear to the garage door, and Shawn did, too. There was barking, growling, and guys' voices shouting like they were watching a football game. Then we heard yelping—like how a dog on TV yelped if someone stepped on its paw. Music was playing, and when the yelping started, it was turned up louder, but it didn't drown out the dogs.

Shawn knocked on the door, but Nick didn't answer. Shawn was breathing hard and shivering, though it wasn't even cold.

"It's something bad, Russ," he whispered.

"Maybe not," I said, not convincingly. "Tomorrow's Saturday. Let's come back and check it out when it's light. We can pay Nick the twenty we have then."

Shawn spent the night in the camper, but we stayed awake, eating peanut butter sandwiches and making something we called camper Pop-Tarts. They're made from saltine crackers, butter, and sugar, all from little packets we got from the DX. Uncle Cory came out to give us two cans of root beer, a new pack of batteries, and a big flashlight. He invited us to come into the house.

"Uh, we're okay," I said. "But . . . thanks."

"All right, but know it's available anytime this camper gets too cold or you get sick of it," Uncle Cory said. "Shawn, your folks know you're spending the night?"

"They know. I asked my mom before I left for school today. She said it was okay."

When Uncle Cory left, Shawn and I talked and rolled little bits of paper into spitballs that we shot at the camper ceiling with some leftover straws.

"Russell, where's that dog gonna live once we get him?" Shawn asked. "My mom won't let a dog in the house. She said that she has enough trouble feeding my dad and all of us, let alone a dog. And besides, our house is too small."

I nodded. Shawn's house was half a house, actually, with one family upstairs and Shawn's family downstairs. Their half had three bedrooms. Shawn's mom and dad had one bedroom. Shawn's oldest brother, Travis, had another bedroom, since he helped out with the rent sometimes, and the other five boys had the last bedroom—with two sets of bunk beds jammed side by side and a cot. Shawn slept on the cot, which made him a good target for his brothers' feet and elbows.

Shawn's mom was short like a kid, but she was the serious type, all fast moves and hard work. But whenever she'd see me, she'd flash a smile like Shawn's, give me a quick squeeze, and hold my cheeks with hands that smelled clean, like she'd been scrubbing with bleach. Then off she'd go, and in one breath she'd tell Shawn's brother to quit clipping his toenails in the kitchen, or Shawn's dad that it was time for his medicine, or Shawn that his math teacher called and he was going to have to go to summer school if he didn't try harder.

Truthfully, I never thought about the dog living at Shawn's. I had always pictured it curled up and homey with me in the camper. For a minute I felt bad I didn't imagine Shawn with us, too. The pooper-scooper *was* his find, and the business *was* his idea. But I needed a dog more. He had a good mom and an okay dad, and he had his brothers, even if they were rotten to him sometimes. I had Uncle Cory. Period.

"I guess I thought he'd stay with me," I admitted.

"Yeah . . . I suppose. But what's Uncle Cory gonna say about having a dog around since he hates them so much?" Shawn drummed his fingers on the camper table, and his voice started climbing.

"What if we did all this for nothing, Russ, and then no one will let us even have a dog? What if we get it and they make us take it to the pound right away? Then what are we going to do?"

Usually I could talk Shawn out of his freak-out by telling him that everything would be okay, or stuff has a way of working out, or some other junk I remembered the guidance counselor always saying when she made me eat lunch in her office "just to check in."

But this time I had my own worries chewing at me. Instead of my mind being on the puppy, it was on those pit bulls and what caused all the yelping inside the garage.

Chapter Nine

 **...**

Early Saturday morning we loaded up the scooper and the bags, got a doughnut from the discount rack at the DX, and rode to Nick's.

Instead of going down his street to his front door, we rode up the alley that was directly behind the garage and the kennels. We checked out the three pit bulls in their kennels first. There were scratch marks on their faces and necks, and patches of fur were missing. One was panting heavy, like he just ran a race. One licked his leg over and over.

When they saw us, they went nuts—barking, growling, and drooling. There was blood on the floor of each of their kennels. I pulled three pieces of doughnut from my pocket and tossed them into their kennels. One dog opened his mouth to chomp the doughnut, and I noticed he had missing teeth.

"Geez, Russ . . . how'd these dogs get so beat up?" Shawn asked.

I didn't answer, but my chest was burning. I was so angry, I was ready to knock Nick's stupid garage over. Or set it on fire.

"We've got to get in there," I said, trying the steel door of the garage, but it was locked. I jimmied the windows, but they were locked, too. Shawn felt every ledge and looked under every big rock by the garage for a key, but he didn't find one. With the lights off in the house, and it being so early, we took the chance that Nick was still asleep. His car was unlocked, so we rummaged through that, too, looking for a key. A letter with his name on it dropped out on the ground, and I popped it back in the car. I glanced at the name and tried to remember that it said "Nick Vaughn," in case I ever needed to know his full name. Shawn found a bag of peanuts under the seat and started munching them.

"The only way we're getting in is if Nick lets us in," I said.

"Uhh . . . have you noticed what a major jerk he is?" Shawn squeezed the handle of his pooper-scooper and tried to change the subject. "Think we should get to work? We've only got today to get the rest of the money."

"Yeah, I guess," I said, but my heart wasn't in it. I hopped on Shawn's bike, and we went back to our regular customers.

While we were scooping up after the four golden retrievers, I had an idea.

"I'll bet Uncle Cory could get into that garage."

Shawn stared at me. "You're kidding, right?"

"I'm serious. All he can say is no if he doesn't want to do it."

"Yeah—after he does a good beat down on you," Shawn grumbled. I ignored him. I'd heard that Uncle Cory may have done a few beat downs in his past, but he never laid a finger on me.

We finished working, and later that afternoon I counted the money. Thirty-two dollars—only eight to go. Shawn rode me home, and I decided right then that I would talk to Uncle Cory. I saw his motorcycle in the driveway, and a light was on in the kitchen, too.

"I'm going in with you," Shawn said. He stood up tall, and I saw his bellybutton because his shirt was too little. It was hard to take a guy serious when you were looking at his bellybutton.

"You sure?"

He nodded.

Shawn and I slid into Uncle Cory's house, where he sat at the kitchen table working on a motorcycle part. He had an old tan tarp over the table and a lamp with the shade off that was pointed right at the part, like it was getting its appendix out or something. An owner's manual was propped open with his elbow, and he was scowling as he read.

I cleared my throat, wondering if he would notice, but he didn't. Then the wrench in his hand slipped as a bolt broke off. The engine part skittered off the table and landed on his bare foot. I held my breath as Uncle Cory grabbed his foot and chucked the wrench to the ground.

My words stuck in my throat like hamburger hot dish. I had to go to the bathroom, too. It wasn't the best time to talk to Uncle Cory, but I had to.

"Hey, Uncle Cory. How are you doing today?"

My voice sounded like a doll that when you pulled the string, it talked. Either that or a robot. An idiot robot.

"Great, just great." He picked up the wrench, slammed it down on the table, then stuck the too-big engine part in the too-small garbage.

"Piece of junk," he grumbled to himself. "Wait till I see the guy who sold me that motorcycle. Liar said it always started. I get it home, and it's nothing but trouble. One bad part after another."

He turned to Shawn and me. "You two need something?"

I said nothing.

"Well, what is it?" he asked again, and he looked at me sharp. For a second I was reminded of Nick.

I took the risk and started. "Okay, well, there's this guy—his name is Nick. I can't remember his last name, but I saw it on a letter one time when Shawn and I were going through his car, looking for a key. It's something like Vosh or Vont or—"

"Why were you two looking for a key in some guy's car?"

"'Cause he's doing something bad in his garage, but we can't get in there to check it out, because it's locked up. And . . . since you're good at picking locks—"

Uncle Cory interrupted. "Who told you that?"

I gulped. "Uh, my dad."

"Well, he's got room to talk." Uncle Cory pushed the kitchen chair back and stood up. He walked to the sink and started washing his hands, scrubbing fast like he'd remembered something he didn't want to remember.

"That was a long time ago," he said. "I was a kid. A kid, trailing his big brother." He dried his hands on a towel.

I nodded. Gave the kind of "Hm, hmm" that kept a guy talking, and Uncle Cory did.

"I've got a job now—you know that. It's not much, but it got me this house and that camper, and neither one of us is going hungry, so I'd say that's all right, for now anyway."

I was quiet. Then I tried another angle. "You wouldn't have to pick it. You could just show me how."

"Yeah, I could do that, but I won't." He started piling dishes in the sink, scraping pans, wiping off the counter. "That's about the last thing you need to know how to do."

Shawn piped in. "But Nick has these pit bulls, and they're all messed up, and we heard—"

"Whoa—hang on. This is about dogs? Is that the deal?"

"It's not *all* about dogs—just mostly about them," I said.

"Then I guess you two are *mostly* on your own. If this guy Nick isn't taking care of his dogs, then call the pound on him and let them figure it out."

I felt my face getting hot. He didn't get it. Not any of it. For some reason I started worrying that I was going to bawl, which I hadn't done in ages. I turned my back and clenched my jaw.

"Just forget it," I said. I shouldered Shawn out of the way, slammed the front door, jumped off the porch, and started running. You couldn't bawl and run at the same time—you had to pick.

Shawn took off after me. He had always been the faster runner, and now he had the advantage of his bike. He caught up. I ran awhile longer until my shirt was soaked with sweat and my breath heaved like I weighed a thousand pounds.

Shawn threw down his bike and then sprawled on a pile of leaves near the curb. He tried talking to me.

"We only have nine dollars to go, Russ! Let's just go scoop, pay Nick off, and bring that puppy home. Forget about those pit bulls. We aren't even sure there's anything that bad going on . . ."

I squeezed my eyes shut tight and dropped to my hands and knees. Once, in that Sunday school, an old guy came in and told us about foxhole prayers. When a guy's in a foxhole, he explained, fighting in a war battle or something, he doesn't have a bunch of time to pray to God with long prayers and fancy words. He says something like "Help me" and God helps him, just like that. The foxhole, the old man said, brings out what's really inside a guy, too—good and bad.

I had nothing left, so I said it.

"Help me," I gulped.

"What did you say?" Shawn asked.

"I wasn't talking to you."

Shawn looked around. "Who, then?"

I didn't answer him, because a thought had started knocking around in my mind about some-one who could help me figure things out. The purple-toenailed library lady named Deb—or to Shawn, his girlfriend.

I stood up. "I'm not scooping any more today, Shawn. I'm going to the library."

Shawn's voice jumped. "What the heck? You've already read every dog book they've got. There's nothing left! Besides, they'll probably be closed by the time you get there."

I started walking toward the library. Shawn didn't move.

I kept walking, and that made him madder.

"Go ahead! Go to the stupid library and read

stupid books about stupid kids who get stupid dogs and live STUPIDLY EVER AFTER!"

I began jogging. Then running full-out again.

Shawn got on his bike, and for the first time since we've been friends, he didn't follow me.

Chapter Ten

 . . .

The library would be closing at 7:00 p.m. I checked the library clock and saw it was already 6:30. I searched up and down the aisles for Deb's shelving cart. In the middle of the picture-book section I found her sitting cross-legged, one hand holding her place on the shelves as she reached for the next book.

She glanced up at me. "Hey, Russell . . . what did you do, run all the way here?"

I got right to the point. "Can you help me get some information? It's real important."

Deb stood up, stretched out her back. "Let me guess. Is it about dogs?"

"I guess so," I said. She studied my face like she was studying a new book. Her smile disappeared, and in a way, I was grateful for that.

"Well, let's hit the computer. Then you can tell me what it is you want to know. We've got a little bit of time."

Deb pulled up a chair for me next to the computer. We sat, shoulder to shoulder, and for a minute I thought about telling her the truth, but I changed my mind.

"Okay. I need to know a bunch of stuff about pit bulls for . . . a report in school," I said, fumbling around.

"That's easy enough," she said. She started typing. "Are you wanting general information, or are there specific things you're looking for?"

"Both."

"Do you mind if I learn about pit bulls, too, or do you want to look things up yourself?"

I felt my face turn red, and I rubbed my eyes to keep tears from dripping onto my cheek where she could see them. I wanted her to stay, and she figured that out.

"Forget the shelving," she said. "This seems more important."

Deb found a site that had details about where pit bulls came from, what they were used for a long time ago, and how they're supposed to be treated and trained. On another site, there were a couple photos of pit bulls that looked like the ones Nick had, before they got messed up.

We kept reading. There were message boards where people said how nice pit bulls were if they were trained right, and other people who were trying to buy or sell a good pit bull. I read bits of articles as fast as I could about loose pit bulls that had attacked people . . .

Then I found it.

"'Pit bulls are the most common breed used in the crime of dogfighting,'" I read aloud.

Deb leaned in close as we studied photos of pit bulls with missing teeth, missing eyes, scars on their heads, necks, and chests. I felt like Terry Grundel had punched me in the gut harder than ever, but I kept on reading.

There was stuff about breaking sticks—something that's used to pry open the mouth of a pit bull when it's biting another dog in a fight and won't let go. I remembered the box of weird sticks I dumped out in Nick's basement.

Everything was there on the screen . . . how people sometimes build a fighting ring with hay bales, how they keep their doors and windows covered so no one knows, how other people come to see the fight, betting money or drugs. There was even something about rottweilers and other breeds used for dogfighting, too.

"How can they do it?" I said, sweat covering my forehead.

Deb shook her head. "I don't get it either, but people will do a lot of things for money or drugs. Maybe someone sick enough to pit one dog against another gets hooked on the feelings of power and control they get from owning a tough fighting dog. It's wrong on so many levels, Russ, and it's against the law, which it should be."

"What happens to the dogs if the guy gets busted?"

"From what I've read, Animal Control takes them, and most of the time, the dogs aren't adoptable and have to be put down because they've been used for fighting."

There was an announcement that the library was closing, and one by one, the lights were turned off.

Deb now had a line of worry between her eyebrows. She put her hand on my arm and talked low. "Russell, what's going on? Why do you really want to know all this?"

"It's . . . just for my report." I kept my eyes

down. I didn't tell her about the puppy or only owing Nick eight dollars more or anything that we heard in his garage.

"Well, make sure you include in your report that most pit bull owners don't fight their dogs."

I nodded.

"Let me know how it turns out, okay?" Deb said. Then she smiled a bit. "Oh, and tell Shawn I said hi."

On the walk home, it was dark, and fat drops of rain began to hit my face. I hunched down and jammed my hands in my pockets. Then I got a crazy thought that wouldn't give up.

What if I let them go?

I started running again . . . through backyards, down the alleys, all the way to Nick's. The house lights were on, and his car was in the driveway, but the garage windows were pitch-black.

I stayed low to the ground and crept along the hedges so Nick wouldn't spot me. Thunder rumbled, and the wind picked up. I thought of the night I was in the camper, and how God blew the camper door open. Back then I hardly had the guts to hope that what the Sunday school teacher said a million times was true. That God wasn't just looking down from heaven, or swirling around in the breeze like a good idea, but He was *with* me, crawling along in the dirt.

The pit bulls were huddled in the corners of their kennels, curled up. When they saw me, two of them barked and charged their kennel gates, forgetting that I had ever shared my doughnut with them. I had a cracker in my pocket from lunch, and I broke off pieces to throw through the fence. Then I tossed a bit into the kennel that had a pit bull who looked too sick to even stand.

I heard something. Someone was coming up from the alley behind the garage. I squatted down in the muddy space between the garage and the kennels—while two of the pit bulls barked and bit at the fence to get at me.

"Russell, you back here?"

It was Shawn, talking a mile a minute. "I did it, Russ! I got the rest of the money—eight dollars! After you went to the library, I kept scooping by myself, and I went to this one house, and they had three German shepherds. The yard was crazy messy, and I told the owner it would be fifty cents a scoop. She didn't even argue! So I did one yard and I made ten dollars! I spent one of the extra bucks on cheez-whirlz, but I saved you half the bag, right here," he said, patting his pocket.

I grabbed him by the shirt collar and pulled him down. "Shhh . . . You did good, Shawn, you really did. But you gotta help me do something, and we gotta do it quick."

"What? What are you talking about?"

"We gotta get these pit bulls out of here. Nick's using them for fighting, and now they're sick and getting meaner every day. They're gonna die, either in the fight or because of the fight, unless we let them go."

"Let them . . . loose?"

"There could be a fight tonight. We might be their only chance."

Shawn rubbed his face hard. "Man, Russell, I got the rest of the money in my hand—"

"I know, but we gotta wait on that a little. C'mon, Shawn, just go along with this . . . please."

Shawn groaned and rolled his eyes. It was as good as a yes.

I jumped up and grabbed the handle on the first gate, but Nick had wired them all shut. Shawn took the end of the wire and started to unwrap it as quick as he could. One of the pit bulls was snarling at us, his lip curled like he had eaten something bad. The other paced back and forth, nervous and meaning business. The sick pit bull just breathed heavy, its scarred-up muzzle resting on its paws.

Shawn had the wire unwrapped, and he began to lift the latch of the first kennel. He stopped—like some idea had just plopped right into his brain, like a rock in a pond.

"Russ, if we let these dogs out of their kennels, what are they gonna do?"

"I don't know—run away?"

"Think about it," Shawn said, talking slow, like I was in kindergarten. "We're out here, and they're in there—acting like they want to tear us apart. We let them out, and what's the first thing they're gonna want to do?"

"Oh."

"That's right. They'll get us. And because there's two of them and two of us, we won't be able to save each other's life, either. We'll both be dead."

I pictured us both in our caskets—neither of us able to bawl our eyes out at the other one's funeral.

Then I came up with what I thought was a solution.

"But what if we climbed on top of the kennel and I hung on to your feet and you could open up the kennel gates upside down?"

Shawn thought about it. Most of the time, he was all about hanging upside down. "You won't drop me, right?"

"I promise." I spit on my hands and rubbed them together just to show Shawn how ready they were to hang on.

Shawn hitched his foot into the kennel fence, reached, and pulled himself onto the rusty tin of the kennel roof. I followed him. With each move, the tin popped and cracked. It sank in the middle with our weight, too. Through a space between the tin sheets we could see the two pit bulls look up and growl. They were on to us.

"Okay, grab on," Shawn said as he laid down on his belly and crawled toward the end of the tin.

I lay on my belly, too, flat against the cold tin, and hooked my shoes over the other edge of the roof as a brace. I grabbed Shawn around his ankles as he began using his hands to scale down the kennel fence toward the first gate latch.

"Don't start itching anything while you're hanging on to me, okay? I mean it," Shawn said over his shoulder.

"I've got you," I said.

Through the split in the roof I could hang on and still see Shawn feeling his way down the kennel fence. When the pit bulls started to gnaw at the fence, wherever his fingers were, Shawn tried to make his hands flat. The half bag of cheezwhirlz dropped out of his pocket. Sweat dripped down between my eyes, and for a minute I wanted to wipe it.

Shawn now had his hand on the kennel gate, when I heard two things—the back door of the house opening and Nick's ragged cough.

Shawn heard it, too. "Pull me up, Russell. Pull!"

I pulled as hard as I could as Shawn climbed his way back up the kennel. The two pit bulls were jumping at him, snapping at the fence, fierce as ever.

Shawn stretched out next to me on the roof.

"Stay still," I whispered. Neither of us breathed. Shawn had ahold of my shirt, which meant things were real bad.

I pointed at the split in the roof to show Shawn, and we watched Nick walk toward the kennel. He had Princess with him. She looked skinnier, and she too had scratch marks on her head and a patch of raw-looking skin on her neck. Nick picked up the wire that had dropped to the ground, kicked the bag of cheez-whirlz, and started looking around.

He dropped the leash and told Princess, "Git him," and Princess got to work, first crunching the scattered cheez-whirlz, then sniffing out bushes, tearing over to a pile of boards that someone could be hiding under, jumping up on an old burn barrel in case the culprit was there. Both she and Nick looked everywhere but up.

The pit bulls crowded their gates, barking. Nick kicked the kennel fence, and they gave a short yelp. The tin rattled with the kick, and I gripped the edge as best as I could without my fingers showing.

Nick got the kennel door open, and we saw him leash up each dog, dragging the sick one to its feet. With one hand, he had the leashes of all three pit bulls. With the other, he had Princess. Two cars had pulled up in the driveway, and Shawn's teeth were chattering from a mixture of fear and cold.

I heard a third car pull up, and then the shuffling feet of a bunch of people, all headed to the garage. Nick and the pit bulls, along with Princess, were now inside, too, and the garage door was shut.

Shawn hissed in my ear. "Let's get out of here."

"Wait. We gotta figure something out."

My mind raced. If we went to the police, they'd bust Nick, but all the dogs would be taken to Animal Control, including the rottweiler puppies. Right now, the house was empty, and between Shawn and me, we could sneak right in, throw the rest of the money on the table, grab our puppy, and set out running.

From inside the garage, we heard barking, howling, and that sickening yelping that went right through me. I thought about all the hard work, the money, wanting that puppy so bad, and getting so close . . .

"Should we do it? Go get that puppy?" I asked Shawn, wanting him to make the decision.

Shawn's eyes were wild. "Yeah, it's ours! Not like we're stealing it or anything!"

The yelping and barking continued. A guy's voice cheered. Someone turned the music up loud to cover the dogs. Then the rain let loose, hitting the tin roof and soaking us in seconds. I was paralyzed.

Shawn grabbed my shoulders and shook them. "Russell—what do we do? Do we go and get our puppy or not?"

Jagged lines of lightning shot around us. Shawn had a thing about lightning.

"We're going to get electrocuted up here! You know that, don't you? And if you get electrocuted first, and I'm hanging on to you, then we're both going down."

I couldn't speak . . . the rain, the yelping, what I had read at the library, and what Deb said about how people fight dogs because they're looking for power and control. I didn't get all that, but I wondered.

Maybe Shawn and I wanted the same thing— a big, mean dog to make us seem tougher and in control.

I knew right then that it had to stop. I had had it all wrong. I hadn't seen that the dog I expected to protect me also needed to be protected.

"I'm going to the police station."

Shawn moaned. He turned his back to me and pulled the hood of his sweatshirt over his head, hiding from the lightning and from doing the right thing.

I waited.

Shawn gave a forced, fast sigh. "I'll pedal—just tell me where to turn."

We climbed off the back side of the roof carefully, but as we almost reached the ground, a pickup truck drove up the alley behind the garage, and we were caught in its headlights. The engine revved. Someone had seen us.

We jumped onto Shawn's bike.

"GO!" I shouted.

Shawn rode like he'd never ridden before, but the pickup followed us down the alley, sloshing through mud holes and around the corners, cutting through the parking lot—right on our tail. We couldn't go fast enough.

Then Shawn came down a curb and we landed hard. The front wheel popped off, and the fork of the bike ground into the cement. It threw both of us off the bike and onto the street. Shawn landed on his arm, and I smacked my head. The pickup pinned us, and though it was blurry, I saw the guy inside the truck get out.

After that, the world turned black.

Chapter Eleven

 ...

I woke up with my head killing me. I was in a hospital room.

Shawn and his mom were there, squeezed into one plastic recliner. Shawn was almost on her lap, eating a grape Popsicle like a little kid. He had a splint on his arm. Uncle Cory was there, too . . . pacing around, then sitting on the edge of my bed.

"Hey, Russ, you want one of these?" Shawn said, holding up another Popsicle. "Some nurse told me they've got a freezer full of them. Kids just need to ask, even kids who are visiting, so that's what I did."

"I'm okay," I said. I lifted up the blanket, and it was then that I saw I was wearing some kind of nightgown. Maybe I wasn't okay.

"You wiped out good," Uncle Cory said. "Are you feeling any better?"

I nodded, but even that hurt my head.

Uncle Cory cleared his throat. "Any chance you feel up to talking to someone?"

I looked at Shawn. He had purple lips.

"Who wants to talk to me?"

"Well, there's a police officer who's interested in what that guy Nick is doing in his garage."

"A police officer. Who called the police?"

Shawn's mom tightened her arm around Shawn's shoulder. "He did," she said. "And he's already been interviewed. I'm proud of him, and I'm proud of you, too, Russ."

I tried to sit up in bed as the memory washed

over me. "Did they stop the fight? Did they bust Nick?"

Uncle Cory patted my leg.

"He's in jail. Animal Control has the dogs for now. The police just need more information."

I thought about that for a while. "What about the rottweiler puppies?"

"Animal Control has them, too."

Then I remembered the bike accident. "Who was after us in that pickup?"

Uncle Cory swallowed and rubbed the back of his neck. "That was me. Remember my motor-cycle's in the shop? I borrowed the truck from a buddy at work."

I nodded.

Uncle Cory continued.

"You two tried to talk to me about the trouble you were in, and I didn't listen. Then you ran off, and I started thinking about it. That's when I went looking . . ."

In my whole life, no one other than Shawn had ever gone looking for me—and not given up.

"I didn't have Nick's last name, but remembered it started with a *V,* from what you told me, Russ, so that narrowed it down."

Shawn had started slurping the other Popsicle —it was orange.

"Are the police here?" I asked.

"Right outside the door. You ready?"

"Yeah . . ."

Shawn, his mom, and Uncle Cory left the room, and an officer came in. I told the whole story, starting with the pooper-scooper and ending with the wipeout on the bike.

When we finished, the officer closed his notebook. "It's a challenge getting enough evidence in dogfighting cases," he said. "But the information you and Shawn gave us should help us build a good case. You did the right thing by trying to get to the police, Russell."

He shook my hand, and I might have been imagining it, but it felt sticky, like he had just shaken Shawn's hand, too.

Uncle Cory came back with a nurse who said that I had to spend the night for observation. She turned to Uncle Cory. "Will you be staying with him?"

Uncle Cory nodded. "Yes, ma'am."

"Would you like me to bring in a rollaway bed for you?" she asked.

"No thanks. I doubt I'll sleep—the chair's fine," Uncle Cory said.

After that, Shawn and his mom came in to say goodbye. Then it was just Uncle Cory and me. It was dark in that room, but I was wide awake, like I had just drunk one of those energy drinks from the DX.

"Russell?"

I turned my head toward Uncle Cory. He was all leaned forward, rubbing his knees like they were aching him. His voice was tight.

"I haven't been taking too good care of you," he said. "You're my nephew, but I haven't done right by you, and . . . I'm real sorry about that."

My throat felt squeezed, like I was going to bawl. "You've been all right."

Uncle Cory shook his head. "All right isn't good enough anymore. But we're gonna get things straightened out. It'll get better."

Uncle Cory moved to the side of my bed then smoothed and tucked the blanket around me. Even though it was dark, I could see his eyes, and there wasn't a shred of anything mean or crazy about them.

It was then that I realized I believed him— because everything he had ever told me had been true.

"Why don't you try and get some sleep?" His voice sounded weary. "I'm not going anywhere."

Uncle Cory stood up. He walked over to the plastic recliner and crumpled down in it heavy, like he had been carrying a big, old suitcase filled with rocks and had just set it aside.

Then, like that, I was tired down to my bones. No more words rattling around in my head . . . just some stuff I was feeling.

Uncle Cory staying awake all night right next to me, keeping watch, protecting me, waiting to see if I needed a drink or an aspirin or anything. It made me think of my mom . . . and it all seemed more than decent, like more than just the right thing. It was like he was saying he loved me.

Chapter Twelve

...

I got out of the hospital the next morning, but the doctor wanted me to spend a week at home before I could go back to school. I still had a headache, but the doctor said that would get better.

At home, I took over the couch and the TV remote. Uncle Cory made me scrambled eggs with hot sauce, and we watched shows together about motorcycles and one about two guys who swam with sharks.

"Maybe you and Shawn can try that next," Uncle Cory said.

I laughed and kicked at him under the blanket.

Shawn went to school and rode his bike over as soon as it was done.

"Man, everyone knows about what we did, Russ. They heard all about the dogfighting, and how you and me got Nick busted and everything. And guess what? Terry Grundel gave me his hash browns today at lunch, and I didn't even need to trade for it. We're like rock stars—only cooler."

"How about Alyssa Clompton? Is she still in love with you?" I asked.

"Even more, now that I'm famous. She and Deb will have to fight over me."

Uncle Cory stood up from the couch. He picked up the keys to the truck he had ended up buying from his friend at work.

"It works better than the motorcycle for hauling you two around," he said, sliding on his jacket.

"Besides, who'd have guessed that a motorcycle that didn't run was worth more than a pickup that does. You guys up for a short ride?"

"Sure," I said. I'd been cooped up so long, even a ride to the dentist sounded good.

Shawn and I climbed into the pickup as Uncle Cory dug out the center seat belt for Shawn. I had the window.

"Where're we headed?" Shawn asked.

Uncle Cory wasn't too much about details. That was one thing that hadn't changed about him. "Been thinking about something, thought you both might be interested."

We drove through town, then out into the country. The road turned to gravel, and dust filled the cab of the truck. Uncle Cory turned the radio to a country music station, just to be funny.

Finally he pulled into a long driveway that led to a farmhouse.

"This is my friend Vince's place. We went to

high school together, and when his parents moved to town, Vince took over their farm."

Uncle Cory stopped the pickup, and a guy came out of the farmhouse. He looked a lot like Uncle Cory, but with shorter hair and tan coveralls. He gave Uncle Cory a slap on the back, and they shook hands.

"They're in the barn. Go take a look, but watch your step," Vince said.

Uncle Cory led the way, and we stepped around straw bales, some fencing, and a bunch of barn boards. The barn was mostly quiet, but I heard birds somewhere high up in the rafters. I looked around, and then my eyes traveled from the rafters to the walls and down to a corner . . . where a box of puppies waited.

"Vince told me that someone dumped them, just left them on his driveway in the middle of the night," Uncle Cory said. "He's been bottle-feeding them for a few weeks, but now they're eating regular puppy food. He said he's taking them to the shelter unless people want them—he's got enough animals out here as it is."

By now Shawn had all the puppies out of the box, not hearing a word Uncle Cory had said. The puppies were the size of small guinea pigs, but way cuter than any guinea pig—with swirly brown fur and some white markings splashed on each of their paws.

I sat on the barn floor and held them one at a time. I rubbed each warm, velvet belly and put each puppy up to my cheek. They burrowed into the curve of my neck, making little grunts in my ear. One chewed my shoelaces. Another one licked his paws like they were something special.

My heart was pounding. I was afraid to ask, but I did it anyway.

I turned to Uncle Cory. "Um . . . you think we could . . . have one?"

Uncle Cory sat down on the floor and leaned back on a straw bale, like he had all day to think about it.

"That's why we're here, Russ. You and Shawn earned a puppy fair and square. You worked for it."

Shawn high-fived me and did a somersault. Straw stuck to his hair. I laughed like someone would if they were nuts.

"Take your time picking one out," Uncle Cory said, and we did.

"Do you know what kind of puppies these are?" I asked.

Uncle Cory scratched his head like he was thinking. "Wiener dogs?"

Shawn threw a handful of straw at him.

"Vince has no idea, actually. Probably a mix of a bunch of different dogs. That okay with you?"

I nodded. Somehow it seemed like the best thing.

I remembered all the stuff I had read last summer about how to choose a puppy, and soon enough we knew which one we wanted.

"This one plays, but he doesn't bug the other

puppies all the time. He settles down fast, too, and lets you put him on his back. That's good," I said.

"Look, he's got a little white diamond on his chest—how cute is that?" Shawn said, tracing the diamond with his finger.

He was right in the middle, size-wise, and he fit Shawn and me like he was meant to be.

Suddenly a poke of guilt hit my gut—not because we had chosen a puppy, but because there would be puppies left behind.

"Do you think maybe some kids at school would want the other puppies, so they don't have to go to the shelter?" I asked Shawn.

"Russ, look at these puppies. Once kids see ours, everyone will want one."

Then it was Shawn's turn to ask a question. His was harder. He turned so Uncle Cory didn't hear him and talked low. "This puppy's cute and all, but remember how we used to want a mean dog to protect us and fight anyone who messed with us?"

I felt my face getting hot. Shame settled around the edges.

Shawn looked at me, kind of desperate. "Do we still want that?"

I was sure of my answer and I wasn't afraid to say it. "I don't . . . not anymore."

Shawn smiled and pulled a cheez-whirlz out of his pocket. He offered it to the puppy, who gave it a lick and then started crunching.

"Me neither."

Vince found us a box and lined it with an old towel. "That'll do to get you home," he said.

Shawn and I said thanks and climbed back in the pickup, and Vince put the box with our puppy right between us. Then Uncle Cory squeezed in. It was a tight fit. The puppy nestled in the towel and fell asleep.

On the way back home, we tried to figure out the puppy's name. Shawn rattled off a bunch of names fast, like he'd been storing them up in his brain for a long time.

"Okay, so I always liked Nacho, Licorice, and Shrimpy," Shawn said, laughing. "But looking at our puppy, none of those names fit."

"Just use them for your top-ten favorite food list instead," I said, reaching my hand into the box to pet the puppy's soft ears. Shawn leaned in and covered him with part of the towel. We were quiet, but then I had an idea for a name.

"This might be weird—" I started. "But you know how we busted Nick and busted up the dog-fighting ring?"

Shawn nodded, so I kept on.

"So what if we named him Buster?" I asked, holding my breath in case Shawn cracked up or punched me on the arm, thinking I was kidding.

"Buster . . ." Shawn repeated slowly. "I like it. I think my great-grandma used to have a bulldog named Buster, but I'm sure she didn't name it that for the same reason we're naming this puppy Buster. Ours means something."

Uncle Cory turned the truck into the parking

lot of Pete's Pet Supplies. The store's OPEN sign was still lit up.

"The puppy—I mean, Buster—was free," Uncle Cory said. "But he's going to need shots and food and something to sleep on." He reached into his back pocket and pulled out his wallet. He took out a wad of money and handed it to me. I had never seen so much money at one time in my whole life.

"What's this about?" I asked.

"It's the money you and Shawn earned. It's not right that you lost all that, after how hard you guys worked. Besides, to get everything that puppy has to have, you'll need it."

Shawn jumped in. "Did you get it from Nick?"

"Maybe I did, maybe I didn't," Uncle Cory said. "Either way, it worked out that I had two hundred dollars in my pocket to give to you."

I nodded quick, not sure I had words to let Uncle Cory know how grateful I felt. "Thanks," I gulped out.

Right then, a van pulled up next to us. I watched a red-haired kid hop out with a big yellow Lab on a leash. He walked right into that pet store, dog and all.

Shawn noticed, too, giving me an automatic elbow. "Hey, this must be the kind of pet store where they let you do that—bring your dog or cat or iguana or whatever right in with you," he said.

I scooped up Buster, who was now wide awake, and gave Shawn part of the money to take into the store. The rest went back to Uncle Cory. He could keep it until Buster needed something else.

As the three of us crowded out of the truck, it hit me hard that something had happened to the dream I'd kept shut up in a box. The dream had changed, it had grown, and suddenly that box couldn't contain it anymore. It did what any dream in a too-small box must do. It broke free. And now, I was following Shawn *and* Uncle Cory into a pet store. I was hugging a warm little puppy, heartbeat to heartbeat, against my chest.